Chemical Wed

Preface

Writing poetry, to me, is alchemy. Take the marriage of ink and paper, together they create an offspring of unspeakable beauty. Words can cause great harm or great pleasure, sometimes both.

Often, poetry emerges fully fledged onto a blank page, other times it has a long gestation and requires much love to shape it into something to be proud of. In my first book Weaving Wyrd, I delved into the secrets of the invisible threads that bind everything living.

Norse tradition says we are assigned a minor Norn at birth, as well as the three Major Norns, Urd, Verdandi, and Skuld, who sit at the Well of Urðarbrunnr at the foot of Yggdrasil (the tree of life) and spin the Web of Wyrd (fate). Their names are said to correspond (loosely) with That which was, That which is, and That which will come to pass. The Minor Norns are not as powerful and can be malign or benevolent.

There are only two things of which we can be sure. We are born, and we die. The path in the middle is way more flexible than we imagine. We can weave our fate with the fate of others, making a tapestry of Wyrd as we walk our path between birth and death. We have choices to make, the only thing that is fixed is that we must make the journey, we get to choose, to an extent, how well we do this.

In Book 2, Chemical Wedding, I continue to explore this theme. Human nature fascinates me, especially what makes some of us susceptible to the darker side of life, while others strive to live in the light.If you enjoy my book, please leave a review, and you are welcome to follow me on Facebook and Twitter.

Foreword

I was truly honoured when Elle Mort approached me to do the foreword for her new book, especially after the success of her debut 'Weaving Wyrd' which I devoured and hope you did too. I have had the pleasure of reading much of her work over the years and can honestly say that the dark beauty with which she writes is disturbing yet refreshing, she will take you where many poets fall short of going. In this book she continues the theme of the choices we make through our lives. From lighter topics of family and kindness to the darker side of the human psyche, she moves through the spectrum of our emotions seamlessly and makes it abundantly obvious that we as beings are neither completely light nor dark. Our choice of paths is our own to take. Elle writes not only for people who enjoy poetry but for anyone who has ever loved, lost, cried, grieved and experienced misery at the hands of others. An honest commentary on the human condition. So read on to find out how life works in its beginning, middle and end. Two of which, as you are here, are inevitable. Not one word is wasted or misused. You have come to the place where darkness rides on the back of beauty. Enjoy the journey.

S C Richmond 2018.
Author of the Alex Price Trilogy

Chemical Wedding

A chemical wedding
of blood and ink.
My inner darkness
merging with the white
of a virgin page.
My desires and dreams
also my nightmares,
made manifest
in the written word,
purged from my soul.

~~~~~~~

He lifted her hair
gently away from her face
and kissed her closed eyelids.
It was not always thus
She was broken on the inside
from bruises and scars
nobody could see
they were inside her soul

~~~~~~~

I am a twisted thing
on the branch of a tree
Hanging there
on a fragile thread
but not broken yet
Surviving day to day
afraid of the next storm
as it may be enough
to send me crashing
to the ground
to die alone
on the forest floor
In my desperation
I call on the ivy
to bind me
knowing it will
strangle me
eventually.

~~~~~~~

One soul for sale.
Not pre-loved
or well maintained

~~~~~~~

It is the colour of the twilight
neither black nor white
In the green and gold of summer days
And the dark of winter's night
It lurks inside the rocky pools
and flows inside the waterfalls
It's in the rising of the bread
and in amongst the dry-stone walls

~~~~~~~

I wandered through the labyrinth
of my mind.
I got lost in the darkness there
for a while,
until I saw a glimmer of hope
lighting my way forward.
For a while it burned brightly
then flickered out again.
Leaving me blind and injured.
I crawled into the darkest recess
and stayed there.
I was surrounded by things
from my imagination and nightmares.
They gave me more comfort
than the monsters who were human.
It was cold and lonely,
yet safer than reality.

~~~~~~~

The band played "Their song".
It assaulted her senses,
like fingernails on a chalkboard.
She was a prisoner in his arms
as they danced.
The music was a dirge
but to him it was a delight,
his held her in his handcuff grip
never seeing the unwillingness
in her eyes.
True love's kiss
had flown away, many years ago,
along with her hopes and dreams.
Bit by bit they had fled
until only emptiness remained.
with occasional episodes
of pain.
She had tried escape,
many times,
mostly in her mind
Like a fledgling, too afraid to fly.

~~~~~~~

Words can taste as bitter
as black coffee
or as sweet as honey
when they roll from your tongue
They caress or they wound
biting into the flesh
like a cat-o'-nine-tails
Then soothing, like a salve
afterwards
Heads or tails?
The odds are the same.
Roulette with words
I cannot predict an outcome
in respect of your behaviour
Wound or comfort
seem to be your only two modes
of operation
Neither coming from a position
of love

~~~~~~~

Cinderella

I sit at the fireside,
staring into the embers.
Once I had a taste of another life
but it was over far too soon.
The glass slippers shattered,
leaving shards in my feet,
when midnight's chimes rang.
I danced in my own blood
until my dress became rags again
and I used it to bind my wounds.

~~~~~~~

Amelie's Lullaby

Sleep now my darling
Sleep in my arms
And I'll tell you a tale
Of a witch and her charms
I will sing you a song
Of the moon she called down
And the raindrops, like diamonds
That clung to her gown
Sleep now my sweetheart
The song is for you
She wove magic spells
So your wishes come true
I will sing you a song
Of the moon she called down
And the raindrops, like diamonds
That clung to her gown
Your eyelids grow heavy
Your breathing is slow
Before the tale's ended
To dreamland you go
And I'll sing you a song
Of the moon she called down
And the raindrops, like diamonds
That clung to her gown
Yes, the raindrops, like diamonds
That clung to her gown

I'm adding a small piece of context here from Amelie's father Brian.

Mearfest is a Rock Charity event like no other It's held in Memory of our daughter Molly who was born sleeping at 40 weeks Following this devastation we raise funds and awareness of Stillbirth and have turned our loss into legacy in an amazing way. We went on to have our beautiful Rainbow baby, Amelie four years later both in our fifties This poem has touched our hearts.

Brian Mear

You can find out more about Mearfest and the legacy Brian and Claire have created in memory of Molly at mearfest.org

~~~~~~~

Natalie

Cousins in blood
yet, Sisters in soul.
A closer bond
could not be made
by enchantment.
We know the secret pain
in each other.
No need for truths to be spoken,
for we are both broken.
Scars on the surface mask
deeper scars underneath
our skin
invisible to the eyes
of the outsider
are obvious to each other.
I see yours and grieve
for not knowing you
outside of my dreams
for so long.

~~~~~~~

I will bury my love for you
In the sands of time
They will stay there
While Kingdoms rise and fall
Never to be exposed
By thought or deed
It will not be revealed
Nor by fire, air or water

~~~~~~~

We were hand fast with laburnum chains
Our souls bound with ivy
The brew we drank to celebrate our union
We drank it from a poison challis
It was bitter with hemlock and rue
Our vows etched in the lichen
Of a tombstone
As permanent as deaths grasp
Our fate was intertwined
Neither of us wanted that
But it was futile to try and break the bond
We tried and failed

~~~~~~~~

You didn't move to take my hand
As I submerged in quicksand

~~~~~~~

You were so pure of soul
That you shone,
like starlight.
I was guided home
by a beacon
that began and ended
in your eyes.
Your arms were the fortress
that kept me safe
from the things of the night.

~~~~~~~

Turn off the light,
as I cannot bear
to see my flaws
next to your perfection.
I cannot hold a candle to you
as you were created perfectly
in the image of your Gods
while I was poorly crafted
in imitation.
If I could take a scalpel
and cut away all
that was unwholesome,
I would be left with only bone.

~~~~~~~

You buried yourself inside me,
deeper than hidden treasure
The seed you planted within
was hope.

~~~~~~~

Slip of the Tongue

Wait
Before you open your mouth to speak
Count to ten
while you think of the impact
your words may have.
Words are weapons
in the wrong hands,
yet in others they hold the power
to heal and soothe
to take pain away
Decide which path you want to take
as words cannot be taken away
once spoken
they can be engraved
into the soul
like a tattoo
on tender skin
permanently scarred

~~~~~~~

The Dream

The night came down
and afforded us
the clearest view of the heavens

We were enthralled
by the beauty of the stars
and the planets

The desultory comets
passed through the milky way
their course set by fate

The fractals of the universe
broke and morphed
into something different
as we watched the sky

A show of light
which although beautiful
terrified us
as we awaited its outcome

The sun became a small dead thing
Blue and cold
We were powerless
and afraid
knowing each second that passed
could be our last

We took our comfort in each other's arms
like two lost children
huddled together for warmth
in an uncaring world

~~~~~~~

The oasis is dry,
the earth parched,
the wells full of sand.
The only water left
is as salty as tears.
All that was green
has become brown
and crunchy underfoot,
like some terrible parody
of autumn.

~~~~~~~

If I could rewrite my story
It would be different.
I could aspire to be something more than I am.

If I could write your dialogue,
you would say,

"My precious, darling girl. You were always wanted and
loved, never think otherwise."

Then you would hold me, so tight, that all my pain would
vanish.
I could take my pain away at the stroke of a pen.
Erase the anguish and edit my story, until you become my
hero.
You would slay my dragons and exorcise my demons.
They are always there inside my head
coiled to strike and catch me unaware.
They would be vanquished, and I would be whole.

~~~~~~~

If wishes came true
I would wish I could love you
The way you love me
But I am untouchable you see
Made that way through
years of being discarded.
Cast away like so much debris,
floating on an ocean of tears.
Washed up in another life
like driftwood on a rocky shore,
I cannot be reached
as I am surrounded by quicksand.

~~~~~~~

The canopy of the trees
blocks the light to the ground
and moss grows thick
on the roots and the rocks.
Even the ponds are stagnant,
still, green things
that are oddly beautiful,
despite the decay.

It is ancient here,
the woodlands older than
anyone living can remember.
The pathways are little trodden now,
save by those who seek archaic wisdom.
Time runs to the music of magic
in this sacred space.

Being here brings peace
to my troubled soul.
It is a place of worship,
a temple to the Old Ones.
The groves grow twisted
and entwined with vines and ivy,
they are home to the ravens.

A monolith is near,
the sigil carved into it,
smoothed by time, hidden by lichen.
I feel its power as I run my fingers
across the timeworn stone.

It kindles my spirit
and makes me whole.

~~~~~~~

A kiss so fleeting
it was borne on
the wings of a butterfly.
It brushed the nape of my neck
as I lay sleeping.
The doors to the otherworld opened
in the mists of my unconscious.
You stood there in shadow,
forged by my imagination,
made real by my dreams.

~~~~~~~

I clothe myself
in a dress of red
the colour of anger
It hides the blood
from my many wounds
and it will become as one
with the flames
to be lit beneath my feet,
when morning's light comes.
My only crime
was to be cloaked
in the green of healing,
of herbs and nature.
I was a friend to the outcast
and unloved.
The hedgerow was both
my bed and larder.
I slept on broom and meadowsweet
before I was taken.

~~~~~~~

The last unicorn
rests in the meadow,
her quest done.
She searched the world
to find another,
but she only found horses
covered in glitter.
They were not enough for her,
She spurned Pegasus
even when he declared
his love for her.
Their offspring would have been sparkling beings
with amethyst horns and wings of spun silver,
but her expectations were just too high.
The Gods wept to see her pride
for hubris was a crime
and her sentence was to always be alone.

~~~~~~~

I took a palette made of wishes
and ground the pigments,
to colour you,
from precious jewels.
I used stardust to capture
the sparkle in your eyes
and the sun, caught in amber,
for your hair.
I fed the silkworms
mulberry leaves of gold
to spin the finest silk
for your gown.
I dyed it with the rays
from a rainbow.
I crafted your voice
from music and laughter,
So you could sing harmonies
with the universe.

~~~~~~~

I sacrificed love
on the bonfire
of my vanity.
Set fire to your letters
the words from your heart
spiralling away in the smoke
They dispersed into nothing
like my hopes.
I chased them for a while
in regret,
but they had gone.
Nothing could bring them back,
but The Gods know how I tried,
to recreate them
in careful forgery
but they were meaningless to me.

~~~~~~~

Would you dance with me if I asked you?
Until all around us turned to dust.
We could waltz into the shadow lands together
Entwined in each other's arms eternally.
The music may be slow or fast
but the dance is the same
always.

~~~~~~~

A Letter to my Younger Self

Do not invite the vampires in,
they are not what you think.
They do not drain your body of blood
but rather, strip your soul
by feeding from your emotions,
and leaving you less than whole.
They can be found everywhere,
not just in the hours between
twilight and dawn,
nor just in the pages of folk-tales
or your imagination.
They are more real than you know
and they lurk around every corner,
just waiting to leach you dry.
I let them in many times.
Sometimes issuing invitations
before they asked for entry to my life,
because I feared them less
than being alone.
Only now I am older,
I see the damage they did.
That they were corrosive
to my life's essence.
They made me less than I should be

~~~~~~~

Some days I wonder
what would happen
if I didn't pick myself up
from the ground.
I could stay down
forever
and never cease screaming.
That is not me though,
but sometimes it is tough
to be a survivor.
There would be few who would understand
even if I had the strength to explain.
How can someone ever feel my pain?
Being a warrior is lonely.
Too strong to take the hand
that reaches out to help,
as I fear that it would make me weak.
I cannot depend on others
as they would soon tire of me.
Scared to the soul
to show my scars
knowing that most would run
and never return.
So I just go into myself,
the sanctuary of apartness
is my realm.
I live among the books and music
in solitude.
It is lonely, but safe.

~~~~~~~

Hope

Her name was Hope.
She was battered by life
and heaped with indignities,
yet still she shone.
Sometimes she felt like
she was made of scars
instead of stars.
But she survived,
and always thrived.
Like fine china,
she was often broken
but patiently put
her pieces back together
and healed herself
by loving again,
despite the pain.

~~~~~~~~

We talked about love
in the starlight of quiet evenings,
always striving for those sacred moments
where we could be together.
It was never to be.
My words were from the heart
and yours, from an oft rehearsed script
which varied from victim to victim.
just enough to make it unique.
You grew colder and moved on,
leaving me, like an unwanted child,
abandoned to an empty life.

~~~~~~~

Trapped in a cavern
made in my imagination,
bound by the Web of Wyrd
to a life not chosen
which I must live
regardless.
The passing of time
marches on,
too quickly.
Rapidly flicking from
one scene to another.
I have no control
over the inevitable ending.
The light at the end of the tunnel
has become a speeding train,
relentlessly moving toward me.
I am tied,
powerless,
to the tracks.
The towers crumble in its wake.

~~~~~~~

I had a dream that you were weeping,
surrounded by people
yet alone.
The waters of the healing well
denied to you,
by those who should have
offered it willingly.
They cast you out of the temple
into the wilderness.
Your cries to be made whole
fell upon deaf ears,
even though you had worshipped
there for years,
they lacked empathy
for your plight.
So, you faced
the dark night of your soul
with only me to witness it,
in a vision.
I was unable to reach out to you
and take your hand.

~~~~~~~

I have travelled through
the Hollow Ways
many times.
The arches made
from twisted trees
as a roof for the sunken ground
made by the passage of time,
and ancient feet.

~~~~~~~

My sins are tattooed on my skin
there for all to see.
I am made of moonlight and magic.
Pulsing with the music of madness,
that lurks inside my soul.

I work in the shadows
and am darker than the wing of the raven.
The ancient waterways
home to my offerings
to the Old Ones.

My soul is made from
the cries of pain
suffered by my enemies.
My kiss is wolfsbane
my embrace is death.

~~~~~~~

I fear the falling tower
I see in dreams.
The parapet is crumbling
with me on the edge.
The only thing that can save me
gone, but not forgotten.
Humanity has become legend,
seen as weakness
by those who should wield it
like a weapon of justice.

~~~~~~~~

I am drawn to the damaged
and the lost,
like a moth to a flame.
I get burned often,
it reminds me I'm alive.

~~~~~~~

The single shred of dignity
that remains,
belongs to you totally.
It is all I have left to give.
You took everything else I had,
all that was wholesome and good
and you left me alone
to grieve for things I've never known.
A past and a future that never will be,
at least not one that involves me.

~~~~~~~

She's a wild type of woman
there are dreadlocks in her hair
and rings on her toes.
She dances barefoot under the stars
and bathes in the light of the moon.
Some say she is feral
and touched with madness,
others say she is mythical.
But she sends spells
to heal them
anyway.
She reads the future
with bones
and runes carved into stones,
her spirit is free and wild
she is Odin's beloved child.
She knows the names of all the trees
they whisper them to her
when she passes by.
Her dresses are the colour of rainbows,
as bright as her aura.
Her laughter like honey
clear and sweet,
you would taste it on her lips
if she kissed you.
The ravens and crows flock to her
and leave her offerings
of feathers and brightly glistening things,
in exchange for her kindness.
She does not fear the darkness,
she embraces it with her soul's light.

She is magic, in the purest sense,
the flowers open with one touch.
from her fingertips.
If she loves you,
it is unconditionally.
Forever.

~~~~~~~

I set you free,
with no hatred in my heart,
as you are too damaged
for me to heal.
The poison in your soul
has taken grip
with icy fingers
turning your heart to stone
as surely as Medusa's gaze
could have done.

~~~~~~~

Love is not profane,
it does not seek to conquer,
it catches you unaware
when you seek it not.
It is like the gentle falling summer rain
not the tempests of winter.
It can be heard in the whisper on the wind
and the cry when you surrender to your passion,
when the tears come through joy and not pain.
Love makes you see the small beauties of the world
through different eyes,
the mundane seems brighter somehow
and the scent of the flowers sweeter.
It calls to you with the softest of voices
and caresses you with the gentlest of hands,
it makes your hearth a warmer place.
It does not exist in the grandest of gestures,
but in everyday kindnesses,
it soothes you when you are weary
and picks you up when you fall.
Love is not profane.

~~~~~~~

Touch my face softly,
trace my lips
with your fingertips.
Whisper my name,
as you softly kiss me
for the first time.
Wrap your arms around me
like a cloak made from pure love.
Enchant me with your laughter,
move me with your tears.
Find my sacred space
at the very core of me,
it is yours to take.
I only ask gentleness and respect.
and afterwards to lay
in the glow of love.

~~~~~~~

Let us go to the stones
as the God and Goddess,
with truth naked in our hearts.
We will lay down together
and be as one,
our bodies moving
to the sacred pulse of the land.
We will feel the waters deep beneath us
as they connect to the pull of the tides
in the oceans, under the moon.
We will be cloaked only by the stars
and caressed by the four winds.
The only fire that will warm us
is the one we create within.
Our passion will open the veil
between the worlds.

~~~~~~~

She offered you a gift.
It was unconditional love,
worth more than its weight in diamonds.
It was handed to you
to keep forever.
She would never take it back,
even if you begged her to.
You were the sun to her moon,
her first thought, every morning
was for you.
She would willingly have
borne all of your pain
if she could
and travel into your dreams
to keep your nightmares at bay.
She would be the keeper of your secrets
but not your conscience.

~~~~~~~

Kiss her
and you will find
her taste is toxic
to you.
My lips taste of
honey and longing
and are yours
for the taking.

Her hand,
burns yours,
like a brand.
My hands will only
be gentle to you
and kind.

Her words are venom,
mine are the antidote
She cries in anger,
My tears will heal you.
She is your nightmare,
I am your daydream.

~~~~~~

What lies beneath
is usually more beautiful
than the canvas
on which it is painted.
Tender care to restore it
is needed sometimes,
Patience my child,
for it will become whole again
but under your
loving touch.
Some of the damage
is visible, to the eye,
some is harder to find.
It is a painstaking process,
but worth the reward.

~~~~~~~

Grief is the coin you pay the Universe in return for the loan
of a precious soul.

~~~~~~~

I chose to follow the raven
and not the dove.
Sharp stones were underfoot
on the seven paths I took
I was invited to a wedding
which was a parody.
The altar was made
from twisted tree roots
black and rotted.
The groom was death,
the bride, decay.
I bore the ring,
to seal their union.
It was made of bone
and borne in on a pillow
filled with rue
and other bitter herbs.
We toasted them
in stone goblets
filled with aconite wine.
I raised the veil of the bridesmaid,
to kiss her lips
before they grew cold
and saw she was the crone,
the virgin grown old.

~~~~~~~

I am the calm before the storm
the gently falling rain
The poison and the antidote
to take away your pain

Your alpha and omega
always the first and last
The child and the mother
your future and your past

The lullaby within your ear
that lures you to your sleep
The arms that will surround you
every time you weep

I am the inspiration
that drives you to your goal
The gentle hand that reaches out
and soothes you to the soul

~~~~~~~

Song for Sandra

It was more than a cake.
It was filled with candy and laughter.
The uncountable sugar strands
we threw at the icing,
whilst willing it to stick,
will stay in my mind forever.
It was made with a well-used recipe
but we added love to the mix
and forged the foundations of a friendship
that will last long after the last slice is eaten.
We share a snapshot in time
of a young man's face
full of wonder, as he cut into it
and the chocolates spilled out.
It was much more than a cake.

~~~~~~~

The gestures I make
aren't grand enough.
For you, they are akin
to dried up things,
that shrivel in your hand.
They flutter and die
before they reach your heart.

I fear all approaches
would be met with disdain,
if I gave you the moon,
you would only want the sun.
But if I gave it to you
it could not warm you
to me.

~~~~~~~

Imagination is a wondrous thing
It's those little flights of fancy
Which will take you to the moon
Without your feet ever leaving the ground
It is at your beck and call
With it, you can walk through the mirror
Into different lands
Castles are yours to explore
From the oubliettes to the highest turrets
There, dragons are real
And you can fly with them
Looking at the land from above
As the wind streams through your hair
You can be the hero
Or the villain
As you like
Find buried treasure with a pirates map
Or fall in love with a tall, dark stranger
It is your journey
A fantasy of your choosing
There are no limits or boundaries
You can throw off the constraints of convention
And be truly free

~~~~~~~

I close my eyes
To sleep some nights
And swirls of words
Crash round my brain
They have no escape
If I do not write them down
They worry at me
With sharp teeth
Until I pick up my pen
And follow me to places
I cannot take them
Nudging less than gently
Wanting to be free

~~~~~~~

Gaslight

Woman, your name was manipulation
You learned your craft
At the knee of your father
He was a past master
And you, a willing student
You knew how to weave a web
To trap all who came close enough
You spun a fantasy of lies
About their lives
To those who listened
When you read from your script
The ability to cry at will
Aided you
Your tears made you look
Like the vulnerable one
You wielded fake femininity like a weapon
That wounded with the deepest cuts
You looked as fragile as a butterfly
In those times
But only those who knew your true nature
Could see your wings were made of steel
And tipped with deadly poison

~~~~~~~

I will not meet you in the shadow of the tower
Lest it should come crashing down around us
Resulting in an cataclysm of epic proportions
With all those around us
Injured in the aftermath

I will not meet you at the shoreline
We could drown in the waters of the tidal wave
When we look into each other's eyes
Quicksand is underfoot
It would be too easy to be sucked in

I will not meet you at the edge of the chasm
The drop is too deep and dangerous
Falling could be fatal
And even if we survived intact
There would be no way out

I will not meet you at the crossroads
It is unhallowed ground
Nor will we meet at midnight's chimes
For that is a liminal time
The bells will toll our doom

I will meet you in the middle

~~~~~~~

The wheel of fortune spins
to be stopped by fate's hand
you do not get to choose
win or lose
You cannot run
from what's to come
Even if the light at the end of the tunnel
turns out to be an oncoming train
the outcome will remain

~~~~~~~

Before you enter my body
you must first enter my soul.
There is no map I can give to you
and no instructions exist,
discover the best path
to reach me.
You need to find yourself first,
for you are lost.
Your moral compass damaged,
some say beyond repair.
But I will help you fix it
with patience and care.

~~~~~~~

I come from a land
of magic and myth
where mist is born
from dragon's breath

Where tales as old
as time are told
woven like strands
to spellbind us

~~~~~~~

Give me your anger
and your passion
before I grow
too old
and cold.

I want to make love
in the thunder and the lightening
not just gentle passion
in the light of the candle.

Let's talk about the universe
and all that is held within it,
rather than waste our time
with the mundane.
I want to stay up until dawn
until our eyelids refuse
to stay open.

I need you to be my equal
and opposite,
not a pale imitation.
We need to burn
as brightly as the stars.
We need to live
in the eye of the storm.

~~~~~~~

Living someone else's life
is a complex thing
Outsiders see another story
to the one fate is writing
for me.
They see love
where there is only need,
and tenderness
where there is only sacrifice.
They do not see
that I have lost myself
along the way.
Duty is a hard shackle
to shake off,
it has left me bruised
inside and out.
I am trapped
in your fantasy,
it is not my own.
Cast in a role
I didn't audition for,
no escape, until the curtain falls.
I cannot rewrite the plot,
circumstances don't allow
for that.
One day, I may have the means
to fly
But until then you hold the key
to my prison.

~~~~~~~

Branches

Of the seven
two are gone
one is lost
one is found
two are damaged
one is broken
If we look
more closely
at the tree
there may be more
we cannot see

~~~~~~~

I built a fairy castle
Filled it with my longings
and my dreams.
In my haste,
I found the foundations
were on quicksand.
The things of beauty
I surrounded myself with
only sparkled for
the most fleeting of moments.
They flickered and went out
like a torch in the wind.

~~~~~~~~

Cherry Pie

She was exquisite
like a jewelled flower
tropical and rare,
with the kindest of hearts.
The first time he kissed her
it was like tasting cherry pie,
the flavour burst on his tongue
like popping candy.
It was the longest summer
he could remember,
a day when he was without her,
seemed like an eternity.
He only recalled this memory
when she was gone.
He'd chased her away
with his indifference.
Time bred complacency
and the exotic had become
as commonplace to him
as breathing.
He tried to find her equal,
looking for qualities she possessed
in others,
never quite succeeding.
He grew cold, as well as old,
while another man was sated
with his fill of cherry pie.

~~~~~~~

In the quietest time of the morning
when you whisper to yourself
"I can't",
but you do it anyway.
That is strength.
that is bravery.
You fight an invisible battle
against the odds
every single day
and win.
It never feels like a victory though
and you never feel like a warrior,
it is enough that you have survived
to fight another day.

~~~~~~~

How can something
you didn't know you had
in the first place,
be already lost to you?
How do you even begin to ask
that it is restored?
Knowing of the loss brings pain
another gap opens
in my heart,
maybe never to be filled.
All I can do is
follow the passage of time
and hope
what I have lost
will find me.

~~~~~~~

The Ballad of a Lonely Child

Even your room
was not a sanctuary.
Never private, or secure
against those who wanted to gain entry
for their own needs,
not yours.
It contained your only friends.
Books, that transported you
to better places,
where there were heroes
to rescue you
from danger.
Sometimes it was quiet,
that made up for the cold.
You were often sent there
so you could reflect on
every misdeed,
but it was never a punishment
to be alone.
It was safer that way,
until the door opened once more.

~~~~~~~~

The first was sorrow,
You bathed in her tears
Your unwanted companion
Throughout the years.

The second one was joy
Her visits were brief
She arrived amidst laughter
Then left like a thief

The third was a girl
And was gentle as rain
She was kindness and knowledge
And healed all your pain

The fourth one, a boy
Was so wondrous to see
He was clothed in the sky
And ran wild and free

The fifth made of silver
Was wrapped round your wrist
Forged by the fire
From stardust and mist

The sixth one was gold
Mined from the land
Given in token
As your wedding band

The seventh was secret

To keep it was brave
You carried it with you
From cradle to grave

~~~~~~~

My tribe are scattered to the four winds.
Lost in time, forever incomplete
only chance can reconnect us.
We mourn the lost and honour them
with the same love we give
to our ancestors.
Some do not even have names
we will ever hold on our lips
for even a second,
but we will remember them
just the same.

~~~~~~~

The Church
became a place of the divine
as the ivy grew around the tower
So dense that only squirrels could climb
I saw decay turn to the beauty of nature
in my dream
The Cross became entwined with roses
which bloomed, scarlet and green.
Graves burst with living colour
and the guardian yew trees wept
to see the order of things reversed
as death made way for new life.

~~~~~~~

The campfire was the only thing
burning brighter than the stars
that night.
The air was clear and crisp enough
for us to be wrapped in a blanket
as warm as our conversation.
We talked of many things,
until the embers began to fade
to a darker red,
like the colour of the falling leaves.
Smoke clung to our clothes
like the smell of autumn.
We stayed that way,
until the pale light of sun
broke through the predawn gloom.
It was watery and uncertain
like life.

~~~~~~~

You walk at my side
every day.
More constant than my shadow,
as you are with me
in sunshine and darkness,
Memory and Thought.

~~~~~~~

I hold the most precious secret
in the palm of my hand.
It is sacred to me,
and will never be told
to another living soul.
The trust with which it was given
changed the boundaries between us.
You became scared
that I would use it in anger
and reveal it.
It saddens me that you would think
me capable of betrayal.
It will go with me to the grave,
even though it was the cause
of the rift between us.
Your fear destroying
all that was binding us together.

~~~~~~~

It's a bleak Cityscape
just the same as thousands of others.
It is built on the bones of the dead.
We walk it blindfold in fear,
the echo of a footstep behind us
in every alley.
Yet there are small beauties
to be seen in every corner,
even in the darkest places,
if we would only look.
But instead we march on
in the footsteps of time
as day rolls into day,
too quickly.
We still forgo opening our eyes
to search its true nature.
The spirit of the place
hasn't abandoned us,
he is in the fountains
and the ancient places
hidden amongst concrete and metal.
In the things that sleep
just underneath the surface,
ready to be awakened once more.

~~~~~~~

Shame on me,
for giving you the power to hurt me,
I should never have opened that
particular door in the first place,
allowing you access to my heart,
unrestricted, knowing you would
be careless with it.
Desires and dreams have held
more import for me,
than common sense,
for all my life.
Leaving me open to
the worst kind of pain.
I hate myself for inviting you in,
but cannot hate you,
as I knew the nature of the beast
which lurks within your soul.
Patterns in history
repeated themselves,
and you became
what you despised.

~~~~~~~

Telling the Bees

We tell the bees of birth and death
To keep a happy hive
What will we do when pesticides
Mean none are left alive?

Without their role to pollinate
The flowers and plants and trees
There'll be no human left on Earth
When we've killed all the bees

~~~~~~~

A lone peacock cries for the loss of his love,
his tail feathers no longer bright as jewels,
they are diminished by his loss.
Somewhere a swan sings a hymn to the dead,
he circles the waters she sleeps beneath.
The book of our life is finished now too,
it can never be read again.
I will remember certain passages
of it from time to time,
and only recall your face in a photograph,
not in my mind.

~~~~~~~

Bravo

Your skills at playing a victim
are fine-honed,
through years of rehearsal.
I raise a glass to you
as you deserve an award.
I cannot tell if your behaviour
is cynical,
or darker than that.
Altogether more dangerous
to the audience you play to.
You nourish yourself
on the pity of others,
whilst having no idea
of how to reciprocate,
or perhaps
you just have no wish to.
People are just props to you,
playthings,
to be abandoned on a whim.
Your supporting cast is fluid,
we are all just bit players
in your saga.
Now I am your critic.

~~~~~~~

This is how limbo feels.
Floating in nothingness,
waiting.
The stage in-between
the euphoria and the sadness,
neither one thing or another.
I want to be spinning
out of control,
because it means I'm alive,
even if I get battered
by the storm.

~~~~~~~

What have we become?
We have forgotten kindness,
There is only love left for ourselves,
If your neighbour has less than you,
you ridicule him rather than reaching
out your hand.
Even if his misfortune has come about
by circumstances outside of his control.
Yet you would expect empathy,
if the same thing happened to you.
We have stopped feeling other people's pain,
if that is evolution,
the survival of the fittest is cruel,
and I want no part in a society
who are self-absorbed
to the point of cruelty.
I'd rather be the outcast.

~~~~~~~

Dirge

The taste of a new name
on my tongue,
seals my new found freedom.
I can be who I want to be,
a blank canvas
to begin again,
painted in my own image
this time,
not in the one you created
for me.
and forced me to live
day after day.
The poet can be free.
for at least a while.
I can write a dirge,
as a final goodbye
to my old self.
An obituary to my current life
my very own torch song.

~~~~~~~

I can connect the dots
and solve the puzzles.
What on earth made you think
I couldn't?
I would ask what sort of fool,
do you take me for?
But that would leave me wide open
to you answering
that I am a gullible fool.
It is true,
but only to a point.
Clarity is cruel,
but crashes in like the dawn
uninvited.
I think I'd rather have been
forever oblivious
to your nature,
and ridden on a wave
of fantasy.
It would have been less painful
than the truth.

~~~~~~~

I will never love you more
than I do in this moment,
it would be an impossible task
to learn how.
You awakened in my arms
and that awakened my soul.
Made me whole again,
when I thought I was broken
beyond repair.
Then suddenly,
you were there,
and my life had meaning again.
We didn't need words,
I wrote poetry on your skin
with my fingers,
it was still there in the morning
tattooed with my passion.
I will never love you more
than I do in this moment.

~~~~~~~

Your touch was as desultory
as your letter,
it lacked the flavour of sincerity,
but still I craved it.

~~~~~~~

Finding Family

The empty places
around my table,
have finally been filled,
with love and laughter.
Just like the empty spaces
in my heart have mended.
I share communal memories
of things I have missed,
over the years.
All the family occasions
both sad and happy times
when I have been absent
are real to me
now I have been given my identity.
There are still chairs sitting vacant,
waiting.

~~~~~~~

On All Hallows Eve
I will dress the table
and set places
that will remain empty.
Three for those
who are now lost
and one in token
for those I may yet find.
I will also set an extra place
with you in my mind.
I will raise my glass
and drink to you,
with love.

~~~~~~~

Another empty night
There have been so many
since you became.
I cannot remember a time before you,
or conceive of a time after you.
Living in the moment
has become both
a dream and a nightmare.
Nightfall until dawn
has become a transitional time
through pain to reality,
unless I dream of you
in my fractured sleep.
You are a shade,
a figment of my imagining
but made more than real
in my life.
I call out to you,
it is unanswered,
you come when you can
and vanish like smoke,
leaving me mourning you.

~~~~~~~

I disperse into mist
I am ephemeral now,
you cannot see me.
I am disguised
by my sadness.
Hidden from view.
I'm not even a ghost,
I cannot haunt the living,
as I haven't passed
through the veil.
but they haunt me.

~~~~~~~

I journey to the gates of death,
where she who comes to meet me
is the daughter of Anguish,
sister to the wolf and snake.
Her face is half-shadowed
but I feel no menace
emanating from her,
only welcome.
She greets me as a friend
and I go gladly,
into her cold embrace.

~~~~~~~

I would weave
the music of my heart
around you,
like a gentle siren song.
Wrapping your whole being,
surrounding you in love.
The tune would resonate
with the music within you,
our hearts would beat time.

~~~~~~~

Charity

We can only spread ourselves so thin
before our cracks begin to show
and we subside into nothingness.
When we reach the stage
where we have depleted our reserves,
there is nothing left to give.
It is then, the voices of those
in need will cry
"Give me more"
and find you lacking,
when you cannot.
Charity learned that
she should begin
at home.

~~~~~~~

Faith

Faith is usually quiet,
except for in the darkest times,
she called out then,
for people to turn to her.
When the guns were loudest
and death was in the air,
Faith was also there.
She was unassuming and kind
but sometimes she was blind.

~~~~~~~

Have a care
how you play
with your prey.
You need to learn
that people turn
into what you fear the most.
When you're on the darkened stair
make sure you are aware
that I could push you down.
When you raise your drinking glass
Think of what could come to pass
with just one pinch of cyanide.

~~~~~~~

I lived in a fairy-tale
once upon a time.
Yearning for the day
I could write
"She lived happily ever after".
It never came,
although it was so close
I could almost grasp it
in my hands.
It was taken away cruelly.

~~~~~~~

What lies beneath the surface is not calm.
It bubbles and seethes with anger,
biding its time, waiting,
Until at last, it gathers momentum to be.
It is full of dark longing and dread,
built from imagination,
and from all the things we cast away.
We cannot escape it, no matter how we try.

~~~~~~~

I was never what you needed.
We passed time together for a while,
on your terms, not mine.
Yet, you cannot bring yourself to cast me off altogether.
I am torn between wishing you would and hoping you won't.
I'm unsure if you act from amusement or indifference.
the resulting pain is the same.

~~~~~~~

I would walk by your side
Until the end of time
Be with you in your darkest moments
You would make me cry
Just to drink my tears
And abandon me to loneliness
We may be two sides of the same coin
But we were minted unevenly
Your edge is razor sharp
I would never tell you what is in my heart
As it would be your focus for my pain
Weaponised for your arsenal
So, I suffer in the silence of my room
And in the chaos of my mind
Internalising and over-thinking
You will never be my companion
Or my friend

~~~~~~~

Overthinking is the playground
for my imagination,
it can run wild and free.
No boundaries to restrain it,
No walls to contain it.

~~~~~~~

It is difficult to explain
The reason I remain
Please don't judge me
For wallowing in pain
It is hard for me to process
What other people do
To sift through all the subtext
And sort out lie from true
Intent, for me, is hard to get
To read between the lines
Needs clarity which I don't have
I can't see the signs

~~~~~~~

I am a Changeling.
Taken at birth,
to a life that was never mine.
A weed planted amongst
the regimental flowers
in a carefully tended border,
destined to be uprooted
and thrown away.
Weeds sometimes flower though
if you leave them alone,
they cannot change
into hothouse flowers,
nor would they want to.
Orchids grow wild,
but they are taken too.
Stolen away by private collectors,
and stifled.
I want to grow.

~~~~~~~

What can I do with my anger?
Roll it in a ball and throw it away?
It would explode, taking out all in its radius,
leaving scorched earth in its wake.
The anger I feel is for myself,
it will implode if I hold it for much longer,
laying waste to me.
It is nuclear, and the radiation is poisoning me,
the fallout may poison you too.

~~~~~~~

What if........?

What if wishes came true?
I'm not sure if I found a Genie,
I would know what to do.
What if I stop evoking the dead
in my head?
Would I ever have closure?
What if I wasn't a poet?
Would I be able to control,
the words that churn in my soul?

~~~~~~~

I was too afraid to fly,
I didn't even try.
My wings are stunted
from disuse.
I tried them out one time
when nobody was watching,
they shimmered with expectation,
but they never opened fully.
Even though the wind was at my back
I failed to take the first step from the ledge.

~~~~~~~~

Roots go deeper than we know.
They grow under our skin, in our DNA.
Twisting and burrowing into our souls.
Connecting the past and the future,
binding us like tendrils of ivy or vines.
We are wed by blood,
that bond can never be torn away,
by time, distance or separation.

~~~~~~~~

There was always something
wild about Eawynn
The way her hair was untamed
and her eyes sparkled
with anger and delight.
She made my heart flutter
when I heard her laughter,
it was infectious and musical,
like playing strings on a harp.
Eawynn made angels in the snow
when it fell like confetti in the forest.
She never felt the cold like you or me.
She was made of all four seasons,
her hair was the colour of autumn,
her skin as white as winter.
She was awake with the dawn
and she danced underneath the stars.

~~~~~~~

I will store memories in your blood,
You will be stirred by the phases of the moon
and the turning of the seasons,
as were all who came before.
Your father and I will give this gift to you,
as did their mothers and fathers before,
it is written in code,
so none can steal it from you.
It is yours alone,
it tells the story of your ancestors
since time immemorial.
We are all here with you,
with every step you take
on your journey.
The strength you have, to face obstacles
we have instilled within you.
We are in your laughter
and your tears,
silent witnesses
throughout the years.
Sleep well, my beloved child,
our love for you runs through your veins.

~~~~~~~

My love is lamented
Mourned as one lost
My heart breaks more each day
He does not come
Lost in my loneliness
With no escape
My mind whirring with questions
As to why he has forsaken me
No answers come to me
However hard I yearn to hear them
There probably are none

~~~~~~~

I will get up in the morning
Put lipstick on and comb my hair
Acting like I just don't care
Reality is different
But the mask will remain
And I will mostly refrain
From thinking about you

~~~~~~~

Grace

When you walk into a room,
you light it up with your smile.
The scent of honeysuckle
follows in your wake,
sweet and heady,
like my passion for you.
The light within you
is reflected in your eyes,
they shine with kindness
and with care.
You fight for the underdog
and give healing to the sick
with your gentle touch.
Even though you are in need
of compassion yourself,
you set that aside
to be a champion for others.
Your soul is bruised
when you feel the pain
of others,
but even that doesn't stop you
from giving everything you have,
when sometimes it leaves you
exhausted on the floor.
You are moonlight on a cloudy night,
and rain on parched flowers.
You grace every life you touch.

~~~~~~~

Her runes were made of ash wood,
from the world tree.
She cast them at midnight's chime,
seeking wisdom and truth
and the knowledge to use both wisely.
They showed her a door to which
she had always had a key
and gave her the courage to unlock it.
The door opened with hinges like oiled silk,
and she found all things in her imagination,
made manifest.
There were books which told the truth
of the fables she had read,
she devoured them without mercy
or gentle handling.
They were hers now to do with as she pleased.
She made the forms of spells with her fingers,
manipulated matter and transmuted will.
Sparks flew from her wand as she wielded it.
She could make flowers grow
and read the stars to navigate at night.
the building blocks of magic,
were hers to command.

~~~~~~~

The atmosphere was sinister,
the table set for three.
Only two were living souls,
the third chair was for me.

~~~~~~~~

All my crying is internal
The tears are choking me
But I will not speak of my pain
Aloud
Pity is not my chosen bedfellow
Although sometimes I wish
I could shout it away
Scream without stopping
Until I was healed
But I will not
I refuse to voice my anguish
For fear you would think less of me

~~~~~~~

I am Blessed

Today I am blessed.
Sometimes it is hard
to remember why,
but in moments like this
it hits me with a clarity
that is crystal in intensity.
Things are more beautiful
in this moment of realisation,
even the mundane sparkles,
like fairy lights on a tree.
The grass is greener
and the skies bluer.
Love creates that illusion,
like a rainbow.
But it is enough
that is seems real
and lends colour,
to the grey of my life.

~~~~~~~

The night was thinly veiled,
drawing us into the mist.
Time stood still in that moment,
in that liminal space.
We didn't fear the darkness,
nor cast about for any other light,
the moon was enough for us,
pale and pregnant with longing.
We felt those who had passed before,
brushing against us,
like they were made of the breeze.
They touched us
and we bathed in their love.

~~~~~~~

I set my crystals in a pattern
on my altar,
seven points in a star,
around my obsidian mirror.
Black Tourmaline and Tigers Eye
will protect me,
Rose Quartz to attract love,
Blue Lace Agate for gentle energies,
with Labradorite and Moonstone
for prophetic dreaming.
I place a shard of Merlinite among them,
it is the key to the door
of the Otherworld.

~~~~~~~~

The air was heavy with the scent of lilac and jasmine,
to cover the smell of death.
The room was dark and draped with velvet curtains,
as we sat vigil through the last long night.
I held your hand, cold and unresponsive, in mine,
and wished I could warm it again
before you were placed in the freezing ground.
I whispered all the things I could never say in life
and filed them away with a list of regrets,
as long as my lifetime.

~~~~~~~

Broken again,
feeling the pain,
wishing it would stop.
Not knowing how
to exorcise it,
for it is a demon.
I created it,
and feed it,
time after time.
Nurture it in my heart
until it becomes
a monster,
out of my control.
Triggered by
something minor
usually.
Overthinking
gives it fangs and claws,
it rips me open with them
and leaves me in agony,
to mend myself again.
I cannot ask for help
without revealing
my stupidity,
so dress my wounds
when I'm alone.
The butterfly tape
holds for a while.

~~~~~~~

Afterwyrd

Weaving Wyrd by Elle Mort. A sample of Customer Reviews from my first book.

5 Stars

Much of the work is dark and will resonate on many levels but it also speaks in a language that beauty understands, there is a talent in this work that is magical. If you have never read any Elle Mort poetry now is your chance as she's placed it within a binding for your enjoyment. Dare you go there?
I recommend you do...

5 Stars

A rich tapestry of poetry and thought. Elle Mort is a weaver of past and present, myth and magic; creating poignant lines and showing us the light and the dark through which every soul passes in this life.

5 Stars

I love this book. The magic it weaves stays with the reader. Full of emotion and energy. Spellbinding.

Printed in Great Britain
by Amazon